THE
BROKEN
MIRROR

KIRK DOUGLAS

THE

BROKEN

MIRROR

A NOVELLA

Simon & Schuster

SIMON & SCHUSTER BOOKS FOR YOUNG READERS
An imprint of Simon & Schuster Children's Publishing Division
1230 Avenue of the Americas, New York, New York 10020
Copyright © 1997 by The Bryna Company
Illustrations copyright © 1997 by Jenny Vasilyev
Simon & Schuster Books for Young Readers is a trademark of
Simon & Schuster.
Book design by Jenny Vasilyev
The text for this book is set in 13 point Goudy
Printed and bound in the United States of America
First Edition 10 9 8 7 6 5 4 3 2 1
Library of Congress Cataloging-in-Publication Data
Douglas, Kirk, 1916–
The broken mirror / written by Kirk Douglas. p cm.
Summary: After the Nazis destroy his family, twelve-year-old Moishe gives up
his Jewish faith, calls himself Danny, and is taken to New York where he tries to
make the best of his life in a Catholic orphanage.
ISBN 0-689-81493-3
1. World War, 1939–1945—Jews—Juvenile fiction. 2. Holocaust, Jewish
(1939–1945)—Juvenile fiction. [1. World War, 1939–1945—Jews—Fiction. 2.
Holocaust, Jewish (1939–1945)—Fiction. 3. Jews—Fiction. 4. Orphans—
Fiction.] I. Title. PZ7.D7473Br 1997 [Fic]—dc21 96-47863

To Uriela Obst

THE
BROKEN
MIRROR

Part One

Moishe's
Story

"Moishe! Get inside!"

Moishe made a face. "Oh no," he pleaded, "I want to see the parade. Can't you hear them coming?"

But his father grabbed Moishe firmly by the arm and pulled him into the house. "Go upstairs and change your clothes. Right now!"

Moishe was astonished. Tateh—that's what he called his father—was such a gentle man; he never treated Moishe roughly. Why was he so angry now? Something was wrong, terribly wrong.

But then, lately, the whole city of Munich, Germany, was angry and tense. The year was 1938 and people were saying in whispers that war was coming, interrupting their conversations whenever children walked in. Moishe, who was only six years old, didn't understand exactly what that meant.

He went up to his room and took off his pants, still bewildered by his father's strange behavior. Why wouldn't Tateh let him watch the parade? He had plenty of time to get ready.

The marchers were getting closer. Moishe could hear them through the open window, stomping their boots as they made their way up the street. He hurried to watch. They were now right underneath his window. They carried rifles and a big red flag with a black cross in the middle, but the corners of the cross were crooked, like someone had tried to break them off.

They were called Nazis.

His father appeared at the door. "Are you getting ready, Moishe?"

"Tateh, who are the Nazis?"

Tateh hesitated and then patted Moishe on the head. "Later, later . . . we don't have time now. The sun is already setting."

Friday evening was a very special time. As the sun sank like an orange ball in the sky, Moishe put on his best suit and a clean white shirt and walked proudly with his father to the synagogue. Mameh and his sister, Rachel, usually stayed home to get dinner ready.

His father wore his best clothes, too, and so did all the people they met walking in the same direction. Soon they reached their destination—a large imposing building at the end of a narrow street.

Moishe watched, his eyes full of intense admiration, as the elderly men with long beards greeted his father. "*Shabbat shalom*, Mr. Neumann." They said it with such respect that Moishe knew Tateh was an important man.

His father was a teacher at the university—

not just any teacher, but the Dean of the Mathematics Department, and that was a very high place indeed. Not as high a place as being a rabbi, of course, but it meant that his father was very well regarded throughout Munich. So maybe his Tateh could be considered *more* important than the rabbi; Moishe would like that.

Standing next to his father, Moishe, too, felt important. He held onto Tateh's hand very tightly as they went inside.

Now the service started and, to be truthful, this was the part of Friday evening that Moishe didn't like much. The service was long and boring. All the prayers were recited in Hebrew, which he didn't understand. He never knew when to stand up and when to bow. Once one of the old men told him that he was bowing too much. "God doesn't want you to be bent over before Him," the old man said. "As a Jew, you are God's partner in the fixing of the world."

Moishe didn't feel like he wanted to fix the world all that much. Perhaps the grown-ups could do the job that God wanted. But he did want to bow in the right places. He watched Tateh carefully and imitated everything he did, wishing the praying would come to an end, so they would start the singing.

That was the part Moishe liked best: when all the men sang, "*Leha Dodi, Likrat Kala*"— "Come, my Beloved . . . let's greet the Sabbath," their voices so joyful and loud. Tateh had taught him this song and explained that, at that moment, the Sabbath entered the room.

The Sabbath meant that for the next twenty-four hours all work would cease and a special time would begin that was filled with joy and happiness. At home, Mameh would serve freshly baked challah—a special braided bread—and other goodies, and Rachel would set the table with a lace tablecloth and the good china. Mameh and Rachel would also light the candles and then cover their eyes when they said the special blessing. Rachel would always smile so happily when she took her hands away from her face, and Moishe could see the light of the candles reflected in her eyes.

Rachel was his favorite person in the whole world—after Tateh and Mameh, of course. She was six years older than Moishe, and she always read to him out loud and told him bedtime stories that he loved to hear.

"*Leha Dodi, Likrat Kala*," the voices of the men boomed, and Moishe wished his own voice was not so high and squeaky.

"*Lo tayvoshi* . . . Feel not ashamed, be not humiliated. . . . Why are you downcast? Why do you cry? . . . The city that is destroyed will be rebuilt on the hilltop."

The song greeting the start of the Sabbath urged you to be happy. The Sabbath, it said, was like a beautiful bride arriving for her wedding. Moishe imagined her all dressed in white with wings like an angel. At the end of the song, the men turned around to face the door and bowed, as if someone very important had just walked in.

"*Leha Dodi, Likrat Kala, p'nay Shabbat n'k-ablah* . . . Come, my Beloved, let's meet the Bride, come let's greet the Sabbath."

They had just finished singing and were about to continue with some more prayers that Moishe found boring, when a loud crash was heard outside. Some of the men rushed to the door to see what was happening, and then screams came from the few women in the balcony. Moishe felt his father's strong hands pick him up, and at once he was enveloped in the safety of Tateh's arms.

"Fire! Fire! Fire!" The screams paralyzed Moishe, but he summoned the courage to peek over his father's shoulder. So much commotion—everyone was pushing toward the exit. In the crush, some people had fallen down, and others were climbing over them.

Outside, looking impassively at the panicking Jews, stood a cordon of Nazi soldiers holding big torches.

The Nazis had clubs in their hands and hit people who came running out of the synagogue. The old man who once told Moishe not to bow was trying to put out the fire with a bucket of water, and Moishe saw a Nazi soldier hit him on the head. The old man fell down and lay still, blood spilling from his head.

Suddenly, Tateh turned around and, still carrying Moishe, went back into the empty synagogue. There was a lot of smoke inside and flames were eating up the far wall. Tateh put him down. "You have to run, Moishe. Run!" And running himself, he pulled Moishe along by the hand toward the back door that went down into the cellar. Through the smoke Moishe saw the bent-over figure of the rabbi, holding the sacred Torah scroll in his arms as if it were a baby, heading in the same direction.

Together, they went down the dark stairway, and found themselves in a room that was pitch-black.

"This way," Moishe heard the rabbi whisper. They groped along the damp stone walls of the cellar to the other end, to the coal chute. The coal chute was a passageway for delivering coal from the outside straight into the cellar. They crawled up its smooth slope to a trapdoor and to safety.

When they got home, they were covered with coal dust, and Mameh almost fainted when she saw them. Moishe couldn't wait to tell Rachel about the drama he had witnessed. But she didn't seem impressed. She only thanked God that they had escaped with their lives.

The next day, Tateh and Mameh had an argument. Tateh wanted to leave Munich and go live on their farm. Tateh and Mameh had bought a farm close to the Swiss border a month before. That's when the Nazis had passed an alarming law banning Jews from the legal and medical professions and from business. Tateh said at the time that a day may come when they would have to leave the city; a remote farm might be a safer place to live.

Moishe didn't understand why the Nazis didn't like the Jews, but Tateh's explanation— that it was because the Jews had the Torah and the Nazis didn't—only puzzled him more.

Were they jealous? he wondered. But Tateh said they weren't jealous; they were angry. The

Nazis wanted to do things that God had forbidden in the Torah, the book that God had given the Jews at Mount Sinai. The Torah contained the Ten Commandments and said that you couldn't murder or steal and that you had to respect your parents and love your neighbor. If the Jews were gone, people would forget what the Torah said, and the Nazis could do what they wanted. Moishe didn't understand why the Nazis wanted to murder and steal. It didn't make sense to him. But he always accepted what Tateh said.

Now Tateh wanted to go to the farm, so it had to be the right thing to do. But Mameh objected; she said she couldn't believe that anything bad would happen to them. They had so many good German friends—cultured people, educated, decent—people who would protect them.

"Where were these fine, decent people when the synagogue was burning?" Tateh asked, and Mameh fell silent.

Finally, after not saying anything for a long time, she agreed—they would move, but only for a little while, only until the trouble had passed.

And so they moved.

The farm wasn't much. It consisted of a half dozen stuccoed, straw-roofed buildings all set around a cobblestone square. One was the farmhouse, and the others sheltered the chickens, sheep, cows, and the four horses that plowed the twenty hectares of hay and wheat fields beyond the large wooden barn. But even if small, the farm was self-sufficient, which gave the family little need to interact with outsiders. They could grow enough fruit and vegetables to put up in jars for the winter; and when they needed other things the farm could not supply, their hired hand, Fritz—the only person who knew they were Jewish—brought these from the nearby town market. Mameh and Tateh feared that some Nazi sympathizers in the town might wish them harm; Fritz was paid well to keep their secret.

A jolly man, fond of German beer songs, and with a potbelly to prove how he had learned them, Fritz lived a few kilometers down the road and bicycled over to the farm every morning. Moishe liked Fritz, who promised to teach him to ride a horse as soon as he was a little older.

Tateh and Fritz did the heavy work; Mameh and Rachel did the rest, and Moishe was expected to carry his load of the lighter chores. Rachel loved all living things, and the creatures seemed to sense it. Moishe would watch apprehensively from a distance as his sister opened the beehives that stood between the barn and the orchards. She would come out, her face and arms covered with bees, approach Moishe teasingly, and laugh at him as he ran away, scattering chickens underfoot. The bees never stung her, but Moishe wasn't at all sure they wouldn't sting him. He'd rather get out of the way, just in case.

Most of the time, Moishe followed Rachel wherever she went; he felt safe around her. And she treated him like one of the little calves she looked after. If Mameh caught him getting into trouble, she could be very stern, and he'd get extra chores or homework to do. But if Rachel caught him, she would only look at him with her soft brown eyes and say, "Moishe, you mustn't do that," and her full lips would curl into a hint of a smile.

Sliding down the straw-thatched roof of the cow shed was strictly forbidden by Mameh. But Moishe knew that if Rachel caught him at it, she would just pretend she didn't see him. One sunny afternoon, he couldn't resist. He was having a lot of fun, until he slipped and fell to the cobblestones below. The shed was low and it wasn't a big fall, but it still hurt a lot. As usual, Rachel was there to save him. She brought him, battered and bawling, into the house, then washed off the scrapes and bandaged his bleeding hand. She promised she wouldn't tell Mameh.

His mother was always quiet. Short, compact, with a round face made more so by the twin braids she wound around her head, Mameh kept away from the animals, preferring the solitude of her flower garden. Her eyes often had a faraway look behind their wire-rimmed glasses as she went about tending her white roses. She never complained, dreaming of the time when they would go back to Munich. She missed the big city—the museums, the theater, the opera. For now, she had to be satisfied with her books and records.

The routine of the farm was peaceful and quiet; yet even here they could not escape the turbulence outside. The radio always seemed to be broadcasting angry voices. Sometimes Moishe overheard things that he did not understand; whenever he walked into the room, Mameh abruptly turned the radio off. Once, as he was helping Rachel carry the milk into the kitchen, he heard his parents arguing:

"Jacob, your friend Dr. Goldman is an alarmist—talking about leaving for America just because he lost his license to practice. Why doesn't he appeal to the courts? This is a civilized country."

"But Leah, different people are leading the country now." Tateh's voice was tense.

"We were born here. We are German citizens," she insisted.

"You choose to forget—they took away our citizenship years ago because we are Jews. They don't consider us Germans. Hysteria has taken over. I think the Goldmans are right—"

"Nonsense, Jacob, I refuse to believe it. These hooligans will be thrown out by the good people. It will be over soon and we will be back in Munich."

Moishe nudged Rachel and whispered, "Are we going back to Munich?"

"Not right away," she whispered back.

"I wish we could go back. I miss school. We never had as much homework as Mameh makes us do here. And I miss all our friends . . . and the games we played . . ."

"Stop complaining, Moishe—I'm your friend."

"You're my best friend!"

She really was his best friend. And he loved her the most when she read to him at night. He would curl up under the feather quilt in the big farm bed they shared, so that only his eyes and nose were peeking out, and watch her with his big brown eyes. She would light the candle, drape her woolen shawl around her shoulders, and reach into the bookshelf by the bed.

"Read the story about Satan's mirror," he'd beg. That one was his favorite of all the Andersen fairy tales. It told of the horrible mirror that Satan had created to make everything in the world look ugly and distorted.

Rachel would sigh—she had read it so many times before. But then she would smile and do it yet again, each time trying to add more drama to her voice. She also would try to read as softly as possible so Mameh couldn't hear. If they got caught, Mameh would take away the candle, scold Rachel, and probably give Moishe extra homework to do. But it was worth the risk.

"Ready, Rachel?"

"Oh Moishe, don't be so impatient, I haven't found the right page."

"It's page fifty-two, Rachel; how could you forget?"

She laughed—she was just teasing—and then she began.

Listen . . . this is the beginning. And when we get to the end, we shall know more than we do now.

Once upon a time, Satan made a mirror that had a strange power. Anything good and beautiful reflected in it shrank into almost nothing, while everything bad and ugly was magnified bigger than before. The loveliest countryside looked like boiled spinach; the nicest people looked hideous and seemed to be standing on their heads or to have no stomachs at all. One freckle became a big red blotch all over a person's face. Satan thought that was very funny . . .

Then he got an idea. He decided to take the mirror all the way up to heaven and make fun of the angels and even of God. He and his goblins picked up the mirror and started flying up to heaven. The higher they flew, the heavier the mirror became. Finally, they couldn't hold it up any longer and they dropped it. It fell straight down to earth and broke into a billion pieces.

That was a terrible disaster. Some of the splinters of Satan's mirror were so small they were barely the size of a grain of sand, and they blew everywhere, getting into people's eyes and making them see every-

thing as ugly and twisted. Some pieces got into people's hearts, and that was even worse, because their hearts turned to blocks of ice.

Satan was very pleased. He laughed and laughed all the more. And he is laughing still, because there are plenty of those splinters flying around right now . . .

"Rachel, Rachel," Moishe interrupted the story. "Do you think there are any pieces of Satan's mirror here on the farm?"

"Oh no, Moishe, everything is so beautiful here."

"What about in the city? What about in Munich?"

"Oh, I don't think so. This is an old story. This happened a long time ago."

"But Rachel, remember the bad things that happened—remember the fire and the . . ."

"Shh, Mameh is coming!"

Rachel quickly blew out the candle. They heard Mameh's footsteps in the hall, and waited, holding their breath. It was past their bedtime, and if Mameh came in, the smoking candle would give them away. But her footsteps receded. It had been a close call.

The next day, after finishing the chores, Moishe coaxed Rachel to play hide-and-seek. He crouched down behind the coats outside the kitchen door, gleeful as she walked off in another direction in search of him. Then he heard Tateh in the kitchen, and he peeked in through the crack of the half-open door.

"Leah, why aren't you listening to the radio?" Tateh was saying to Mameh.

"I don't want to hear any more." Mameh didn't sound happy. "I want to talk to you."

"What about?"

"I'm not sure that it is healthy for Rachel and Moishe to spend all their time together."

"Well, yes, I think they should have other friends. But what can we do in this situation? To bring them into town is to expose them to prying eyes. Too many people would quickly realize we are Jews hiding out here from the Nazis."

"No, I know we can't send them into town,

but maybe at the very least, we should give Moishe his own bed. He is getting older—he is ten and Rachel almost sixteen—so that would be best."

"What do you propose?"

"Let's make up the loft for him."

Moishe didn't like what he'd just heard. He didn't want to be banished to the loft, away from Rachel.

Later, Mameh tried to tell him that he was getting his own room because he was growing up. He hated the whole idea, but Mameh wouldn't listen to his objections or pleas.

That evening, a crestfallen Moishe carried his few belongings up the wooden ladder. Mameh had fixed up the loft with colorful pictures and a pretty quilt, and she hung lace curtains at the tiny window that looked out onto the farmyard and stables beyond. But to Moishe it might as well have been a gloomy dungeon. The heavy, rough-cut beams of the roof seemed to loom ominously over him as he sat on his cot, hunched over, as if holding up their oppressive weight. A spider ran across his hand, and Moishe, never afraid of spiders before, flinched involuntarily. He wanted so badly to be downstairs again, curled up safely against Rachel in that big farm bed.

As he lay there trying not to cry, he heard someone slowly climbing the ladder. Rachel's head peeked through the trapdoor, and Moishe had to clasp his hand over his mouth to stifle a happy cry. His eyes never left her as she carefully lit a small candle she had hidden in her apron pocket. She sat on the bed beside him and continued with the story of Satan's mirror.

It told of a little boy named Kay and a little girl named Gerda. They weren't brother and sister, but they loved each other as if they were.

One day Kay and Gerda were looking at a picture book full of animals and birds, when suddenly— just as the clock struck five—Kay cried, "Oh! Something has stabbed my heart! And now something has got into my eye!"

The little girl rushed to his side. "What's the matter?" Kay just blinked his eyes. But there was nothing to be seen.

"I think it's gone," he said. But it was not gone. It was one of those splinters of glass from Satan's mirror, the one that made anything good look ugly and anything bad look fine and grand. Poor Kay had a splinter in his heart, too, which would turn it into a block of ice. It didn't hurt anymore, but it was there.

Gerda felt something had gone very, very wrong, and she started to cry. But that only made Kay angry.

"Stop crying!" he shouted at her. "You are so ugly!" Then he ran over to the flower garden, which they had both loved so much, and he started ripping the heads off all the beautiful roses.

"Kay, what are you doing?" Gerda was very upset, but Kay only laughed and ran away.

After that everything changed. When Gerda brought over books so they could read them out loud, Kay ridiculed her and said her books were for babies. He didn't want to read together anymore.

"I would never do that," Moishe said solemnly to Rachel, "even if I had a sliver of Satan's mirror in my heart. I love reading books . . . and I would never make you cry, Rachel. Never, never, I promise."

"I know, Moishe. But now it's time for you to go to sleep. I'll try to read some more to you tomorrow."

"Okay, but before you go, Rachel, will you check my eyes to be sure?"

"Check for what Moishe . . . evil slivers?"

"Well, the wind was blowing today . . ."

With a wide smile on her face, Rachel peered into his eyes and pronounced them sliver-free.

Then she blew out the candle.

On Friday evening Tateh always finished the farm chores early. The family washed up thoroughly, put on their best clothes, and sat around the kitchen table, which was covered with the special lace tablecloth they had brought from Munich. Mameh made the blessing over the lighted candles that greeted the Sabbath, while Rachel repeated the prayers along with her. Moishe felt very grown-up when his father let him make the blessing over the breaking of the challah, the Sabbath bread: "Blessed is God, Judge and King over all the world, who brings forth the bread from the earth."

Moishe didn't exactly understand how bread came from the earth, but his father said that it did—not directly, but the long way around. First it was wheat, which was like yellow grass with seeds, and these seeds were ground into flour, which was kneaded into dough, which was baked into bread. Whew! It sure had a long way to go from the earth to the bread on the table.

One Saturday evening, just after the Sabbath was over, Moishe was helping Fritz round up the cows from the pasture when a young man carrying a knapsack walked over the brow of the hill. Moishe had never seen a visitor to the farm before.

"Who are you?" Fritz called out as the fellow approached.

"A friend—looking for Mr. Neumann," he replied.

Fritz surveyed him suspiciously.

"I used to be a student of his," the young man added, coming nearer and showing straight white teeth in a sincere smile. He was of medium height and stocky build, with light brown hair, brown eyes to match, and a neatly trimmed beard.

"Mr. Neumann is very busy," Fritz answered brusquely.

Moishe was surprised that Fritz was acting so rude. "But Fritz, we never get any visitors. I think my father would like to see him."

Fritz grumbled an incoherent reply, so Moishe offered, "I'll take you." He led the way to the barn, Fritz following without a word. Tateh was tending a mare's hoof that had been punctured by a nail a few days before. As they approached, he slowly lowered the hoof and stared intently at the stranger's face.

The stranger spoke up: "Don't you remember me? I'm David Meyer—your worst student."

Tateh's face broke out in a wide grin. He enveloped the young man in a tight embrace. "David, David—is that you behind the beard? The last time I saw you, you weren't shaving yet."

"I'm still not shaving."

Tateh laughed heartily. "How time flies. How did you find me?"

"Your friend Dr. Goldman sent me with a message for you."

"How are the Goldmans getting along?"

"They've left the country."

"It's that bad?"

David, no longer smiling, glanced over his shoulder at Fritz. "I must talk to you—in private."

"Oh, don't worry," Tateh said. "We are all friends here. But let's go inside and get you some refreshment after your travels."

Fritz followed them up to the house; Moishe noticed that he was still eyeing the stranger with suspicion.

Once inside, the family sat around the kitchen table listening to David. "All the Jews from the cities are gone, and now the Nazis have 'Jew hunters' combing the small towns and farms for anyone who's managed to hide."

In the silence that followed, David gulped down a few mouthfuls of the soup Mameh had put before him. "On the way here, I saw Nazi trucks loaded with people—men, women, children."

"Where are they taking them?" Mameh asked. Moishe was bewildered by the tremor in her voice.

"I'm not sure," David answered. "I hear they are being shipped to camps in various countries."

"Camps? What sort of camps?" Moishe asked excitedly, thinking of tents and campfires.

They looked at him, and Moishe was embarrassed that he had interrupted grown-ups talking.

"I don't know, Moishe," said David with a faint smile.

"Don't you think . . . " Mameh's voice was still unsteady, "we are safe here until it's over?"

"NO!" Moishe almost jumped at David's sharp response. "I'm on my way to Lake Constance—if I can cross over into Switzerland, there are ways of getting out to Palestine or America. Come with me."

"Yes." Tateh nodded. "You are right. We must leave."

"But when, Jacob?" The panic in Mameh's voice was increasing.

"Now, Leah, now." Tateh put his arm around Mameh, and she hid her face against his shoulder. "Moishe," Tateh said hoarsely, "why don't you and Fritz give the animals enough hay to last a couple of days?"

Moishe ran out calling, "Fritz! Fritz!" But the hired hand was nowhere to be found. Then Moishe noticed that his bicycle was gone. What made him leave? What was happening? Moishe felt something was wrong; he wanted to tell Tateh, but Tateh was already busy packing. He better do as he was told. He ran to the barn to feed the animals.

He came back, all out of breath. "Pack your things, Moishe. Hurry, hurry," Rachel urged him. Moishe had a million questions, but he was overwhelmed by it all, so he just obeyed Rachel.

He was in the loft, putting his few things in a satchel, when he heard the rumble of an approaching truck. He rushed to the little window, and through the web of tree branches he saw blazing headlights enter the farmyard. Dogs were barking. The truck came to a screeching halt and two uniformed men carrying rifles jumped out. They raced to the front door and smashed it with their rifle butts. He would never forget the sound. They burst into the house.

Moishe's heart was pounding as he peeked down from the opening to the loft. They were pulling out drawers and turning over furniture. He didn't understand why. Suddenly his heart stopped. One of the soldiers looked up directly at him. "*Heraus!* Out!" he commanded. Moishe was too petrified to move. The soldier grabbed him by his shirt, pulled him down, and dragged him out of the house.

In the courtyard, the soldiers were barking orders as they herded everybody toward the waiting truck. Moishe looked up and saw Fritz sitting in the cab of the truck next to the driver. What was he doing with the soldiers? He wanted to call out to him, but Fritz just kept staring straight ahead and Moishe thought better of it.

One soldier snatched Tateh's gold pocket-watch. Another grabbed Mameh's hand. She backed away, trembling and pleading, "No, no, let me go." He roughly yanked the wedding ring off her finger. When Tateh tried to intervene, the soldier shoved him aside with the butt of his rifle. Rachel started to cry. David put his arm around her while Tateh held Mameh, soothing her and repeating: "It will be all right; it will be all right."

Moishe tugged on his father's sleeve, "Why is Fritz with them?"

Tateh patted his curly hair. "People do many strange things out of fear . . . or greed."

Moishe didn't quite understand, but there was such sadness in his father's eyes, he didn't ask any more.

They were taken to the train depot, where a long freight train was waiting. They were ordered to get into a boxcar with three other Jewish families. One of the men said he had been on the train for four days and had heard it was bound for Italy, where a new concentration camp had been opened.

When the train stopped occasionally to pick up more Jews, tin cups of water and hunks of black bread were handed to them through a narrow slot in the door, then the slot was tightly latched. They were not allowed to get off. There was no bathroom, and they had to relieve themselves in the corner of the boxcar where some straw had been piled up, shielding one another for a little privacy. The boxcar was always in semidarkness, the only light filtering through small openings near the roof.

Over the three days of travel, David was the cheerful one, trying to engage others in conversation and word games to pass the time. He took special care to look after Rachel, putting his coat around her shoulders when it was cold, making a place for her to sit when she tired of standing, insisting she share his food rations.

They all bore up fairly well through the ordeal, except for Mameh, who only stared ahead in a sort of trance. Tateh had to coax her to eat some of the bread, but she seemed oblivious to everything around her, humming a Chopin sonata and rocking back and forth as if she were a metronome marking time.

Moishe took his cue from Tateh, who seemed calm and unafraid. Tateh lent him a penknife, and Moishe kept himself busy trying to chisel a hole through the thick boxcar wall. It wasn't easy, and he wished he was as strong as Tateh.

The man who said they were going to Italy was right. Soon enough they were in Trieste, and there they got off the train and were again put on trucks, which took them to the edge of town. When Moishe got off the truck, he saw a large iron gate set in a high stucco wall that enclosed several brick buildings. A sign above the gate read: LA RISIERA DI SAN SABBA.

"What does it mean?" Moishe asked.

"*Risiera* means rice factory," said David. "Maybe we'll get something good to eat."

Soldiers with rifles ordered them to walk through the gate. Ahead of him, Moishe saw a tall chimney billowing black smoke into a clear blue sky. He reached out and grasped Tateh's hand

and was surprised to find that it was shaking; he looked up into his father's face and saw his chin quivering. Moishe felt something terrible was about to happen.

They were marched double-file down a narrow gravel roadway between the buildings and made to line up in the courtyard for the camp commandant's review. The commandant was dressed in a military uniform with many medals pinned to his chest. He was a tall man—slim, not more than forty—and he walked back and forth, spinning gracefully on the heels of his shiny black boots, studying with electric eyes the collection of prisoners before him. His slender gloved hand impatiently flicked a crop as he gave orders to his adjutants.

The Jews, too frightened to object, were quickly divided into different groups. The eerie silence that hung in the air was interrupted by an occasional stifled sob. The ones to be led away first were the youngest children, the more frail of the women, the sick, and the elderly. Moishe saw Mameh in that group. Still in her trance, she shuffled along like a sleepwalker; suddenly she looked so old.

"Where is she going?" Moishe asked, but Tateh just stared at Mameh and mumbled a prayer in Hebrew.

Those who seemed fit to work were next, and Tateh, Moishe, and David were put with them. Moishe looked over to where Rachel stood with other young women and saw the commandant talking to one of his adjutants as he pointed in her direction. The officer took Rachel politely by the arm and led her to a waiting car. Startled by a muffled cry next to him, Moishe turned to see David, his eyes wide with horror, biting down hard on a tightly clenched fist.

That day an unbelievable existence began. They had numbers tattooed on their arms—they were not people with names anymore but objects to be used and abused. They were housed in cramped quarters, six men to a compartment that once held stores of unbleached rice. During the days, loud music blared—Strauss waltzes were the commandant's favorite. At night, an eerie silence pervaded the air, occasionally broken by the clanging of steel doors and the cries of prisoners being dragged out.

In the beginning, Moishe barely slept at all, jumping at each new, horrifying sound. In the morning it was difficult for him to breathe as he waited for the rifle shots—the start of the daily executions. The screams of the dying, which the blaring music could not drown out, penetrated to his bones and made him quiver uncontrollably for hours.

But, as the months went by, an invisible coating had begun to cover his emotions. After two years had passed he didn't even cry anymore when he thought of Rachel and Mameh. The continuous nightmare seemed routine. At least he and Tateh were together.

David was with them for a while, until he was assigned to work in the woodshop. Tateh was given welding work in the basement machine shop, and Moishe was allowed to help him, to sweep up and stack materials.

Moishe wore only the clothes he had come in, now tattered and very dirty. His pants had gotten too short for his long legs; he had grown much taller in the time that they had been there. But his father seemed to have shrunk. Tateh was very thin now, and he coughed constantly.

When he was finished with his work, Moishe would perch on the basement windowsill. Sitting there, he was level with the gravel roadway that led to the main courtyard, the center of the camp's activities. That was where the executions took place. Moishe couldn't see the bullet-scarred wall, or the long, sloped wooded trough to catch the blood, or the bodies being carted away by the wheelbarrows to the crematorium, where they were burned into ashes. Black smoke billowed constantly from the tall chimney.

He pressed his cheek to the steel bars and watched the different feet going past—the clean, high-stepping boots of the Nazis, the sauntering, dusty boots of the Italian guards, the slow-shuffling, worn-out shoes of the inmates. For many months he had watched the passing feet, hoping to see the brown walking shoes with yellow laces that his mother had worn on the day they arrived. After a while, he gave up—he knew he would never see them again.

But one day, he recognized a different pair of shoes—the wooden clogs that he remembered so well clattering against the farmyard cobblestones when they hurried to the barn. They were Rachel's shoes. Rachel was there, somewhere close by!

Moishe was so happy! He couldn't wait to tell Tateh, but his father's reaction was very much subdued. "Oh yes, very good news, Moishe," Tateh said, but he seemed sad. Tateh was sad all the time now. He sat staring into space when he wasn't working, and his look reminded Moishe had of the way Mameh had looked on the train.

"Are you all right, Tateh?" Moishe asked.

His father was doubled over in a spasm of coughing. He stopped, trying to catch his breath. "I'm fine, I'm fine," he muttered and he went back to work.

The work seemed to exhaust his father.

Moishe was worried about him, but what could he do? He sighed and turned back to the window.

A prisoner's legs stopped in front of him. When the legs squatted down, Moishe looked into a smiling face.

"David!"

"How are you, little Moishe?"

"Fine."

"And your father?"

"He coughs all the time."

"I'm sorry to hear that. Take care of him, Moishe. You know what happens when a man can't do his work."

"I'm trying."

"Listen . . . ," David quickly looked around, "this will cheer him up. I overheard the Italians talking, and you know what? The Nazis are losing the war. We should be out of here—God willing—very soon."

Moishe grabbed both bars and pressed his eager face closer. "Are you sure?"

David nodded, grinning from ear to ear. "And tell him . . . Rachel is fine."

"Did you see her?"

"Yes, I'm building bookshelves in the commandant's house this week, and guess what? She works there. She sends her love."

"Oh, that will make Tateh happy."

"And, Moishe," David hesitated, "when it's all over I want you to be my best man."

"Best man?" Moishe repeated, unsure what that meant.

"Yes, at my wedding." He threw a quick glance over his shoulder again. "I'm going to marry your sister." And then his face disappeared from view.

Moishe rushed into the back room, yelling, "Tateh! Tateh! David just—"

He gasped.

Two German guards were dragging away his father's inert body. Tateh had always been so strong and protective. How weak he seemed now, his body limp, lifeless.

"NO!" Moishe screamed, hurling himself against one guard, who, with a sweep of his arm, sent him reeling against the worktable. He hit his head hard, and he blacked out.

When he came to, even before he opened his eyes, he put his hand to his throbbing head and felt a big lump and a strange sticky liquid.

"Don't touch that," said a soft voice, the sweetest voice in the world—Rachel's voice. Moishe knew he had died and gone to heaven— he had always believed Rachel must really be an angel.

But then he opened his eyes and realized that he was not in heaven, but in a very nice kitchen with a glowing oven and a brick floor. He was lying on something soft, and Rachel—real Rachel, flesh and blood, not an angel—was bending over him.

"Where is Tateh?" he asked.

Rachel looked at him with big brown eyes that were very sad, and said, "He is with God now, Moishe. He was very sick, but his suffering is over now."

"But why?"

"We mustn't talk about it."

Moishe wanted to talk about it, but just as he raised his head, he blacked out again.

He was sick for a long time, lying in Rachel's bed, in a little room behind the kitchen of the commandant's house. But Rachel healed him like she always had before.

It was a miracle that he survived. David had told Rachel about the conditions Moishe was living under, and she had interceded with the commandant to give him a job in the kitchen. But when she went to get him, she found her brother lying unconscious on the floor.

Rachel saved him. Rachel always saved him. Even though Mameh and Tateh were gone, he still had Rachel. The war was almost over, David had said. They would all be together soon. David would marry Rachel, and they would be his family.

When Moishe got well, Rachel gave him a clean shirt, a pair of overalls, and a cot of his own in her tiny room. But she let him crawl in beside her when he couldn't sleep, and then they were together as they used to be on the farm.

During the day, while Rachel was upstairs tending the commandant's quarters, Moishe worked in the kitchen. It was a large room with a brick floor and cast-iron stoves, and he sat at the long pine table, peeling potatoes. He also cleaned pots and pans and scrubbed the floor. He liked being in the kitchen. The smell of food was comforting, and he felt safe. And the best thing of all were the leftovers from the commandant's table!

Rachel warned him never to go past the enclosure that surrounded the commandant's house. But whenever he went to the woodshed, he couldn't help peering through a knothole in the fence. He would watch the emaciated Jews of the camp as they shuffled about in their rags. Often he would throw pieces of bread that he stole from the kitchen over the fence and then quickly run back into the house.

One night he asked, "Rachel, do you think the commandant has a piece of Satan's mirror in his heart?"

"No, Moishe, I don't think so." Rachel paused, as if weighing what to say next. "I feel sorry for him. He's a soldier—from a long line of military officers. He is only following orders."

"But they are killing people here."

"This is war, Moishe—that's what they do when they capture enemy soldiers."

"The Gypsies that are here, they are enemy soldiers?"

"I don't know. Maybe some of them are."

"But we are not enemy soldiers," Moishe persisted. "What about people like us?"

Rachel's voice was hardly above a whisper. "We're here because we're Jews."

For a long time nothing was said; then Moishe broke the silence. "Let's not be Jews."

"What are you talking about?"

"You just said it—we're here because we are Jews. So, let's not be Jews."

"We were born Jews. You were named after Moses, our great leader. We will always be Jews. Now go to sleep."

Moishe pulled the covers tightly around him. He looked up into the darkness and thought, *I don't want to be a Jew.* He hoped that Rachel couldn't hear his thoughts.

It was spring 1945. The war was almost over.

The American troops were getting closer. The Italian guards of the camp were tense, whispering among themselves. Friction developed between them and the Germans. The commandant speeded up the schedule of executions. The crematorium was now in operation around the clock and smoke billowed out day and night.

Moishe's routine continued. He was planting tomatoes in the garden, patiently digging a little hole for each individual seedling, when the usual quiet of the camp was interrupted by the din of loud voices. He peered through the hole in the garden fence and saw prisoners scurrying from one barracks to another. What was happening?

Frightened, Moishe grabbed his basket of seedlings and hurried back toward the kitchen. He was almost knocked down by two Italian guards, babbling and gesturing as they rushed toward a truck at the camp gate. The commandant's Mercedes-Benz was waiting in front of the house, the motor idling, the driver behind the wheel.

Suddenly, David was running toward Moishe,

yelling, "We're free! We're free! The Americans are down the road!" He grabbed Moishe, who was still holding his basket, picked him up, and kissed him on both cheeks. "We're free, Moishe! We've survived!"

Putting him down, David asked, "Where is Rachel?"

"She must be inside."

David ran toward the front of the house, but just then the door opened and the commandant emerged. Rachel was behind him in the hallway.

The commandant saw David rushing toward him and with a cold, steely glance raised an outstretched arm, pointing it at David. There was a gun in his hand. Moishe stood transfixed.

"NO!" Rachel screamed as she grabbed the commandant's arm. He whipped around and knocked her to the ground. The gun exploded. Moishe watched Rachel try to get up, then stumble and fall, and lie still.

Meanwhile, David had thrown himself on the commandant's back and knocked him to the ground. The two bodies—one in rags, the other in a neatly tailored uniform, rolled around on the ground.

The commandant's driver jumped in and pulled David away. Again, the commandant's gun exploded. This time it was David who fell.

The commandant got up, straightened his uniform, calmly stepped over David and got into his car. Moishe stood rooted to the spot as the car roared past him. His heart was pounding wildly.

From the camp, he could hear the happy cries of the Jews who had survived. But he didn't care. His life was over. Everyone he had loved was gone.

The Americans finally entered the camp.

Moishe's little hand seemed lost in the strong grasp of a large black soldier with a smiling face, who led him out of the madness. The American tried to communicate by pointing his finger at Moishe's chest, "Jew?"

Moishe froze.

The soldier raised his voice as if Moishe was

hard of hearing. *"Jude?"* He used the German word this time.

"No," Moishe lied, shaking his head.

The soldier didn't understand; he looked at Moishe questioningly.

Moishe pointed at himself. *"Zigeuner."*

"Zigeuner? Ahh . . . Gypsy." The soldier had obviously picked up some German. "Your name—*nah-me?* " he asked.

"Daniel," said Moishe, remembering one of the Gypsy boys at the camp.

"Oh, Danny-boy," the soldier sang, grinning.

Moishe was almost thirteen. It was almost time for his Bar Mitzvah, the ceremony that would make him a man. But he was no longer a Jew.

Part Two

Danny's
Story

From the day that Tyrone walked him out of San Sabba, Moishe—now known as Danny—and his new American friend had been together. At first Tyrone meant to load him onto the big army truck with the other liberated concentration camp prisoners, but Danny grabbed the soldier's uniform and clung to him desperately.

"You're going to a nice place—don't be afraid,"

Tyrone tried to reassure him. But Danny, remembering the truck that had taken his whole family away from the farm, just clutched harder. The Marine stooped to reason with him, but Danny's eyes registered only terror.

"The hell with it," Tyrone finally said, tossing the boy over his shoulder and jumping aboard his green Jeep. He took Danny with him to a small abandoned hotel, where his all-black paratrooper squad was headquartered. The lieutenant in charge pretended not to see this little white stowaway sticking out among his men.

Danny became center of the squad's attention; now that the war was over they had a lot of free time. Each one of the Marines undertook some project to help Danny. Tyrone got him some decent clothes—a couple of pairs of blue jeans and some sweatshirts. Sam, the squad cook, took special interest in Danny's malnourished appearance, and made it his personal challenge to prepare foods the boy would like. But Danny didn't have much of an appetite.

Sam would not be deterred. One day he got

Danny to finish a plateful of spaghetti by show-ing him how much fun it was to suck the noodles up through a straw. Then he staged a contest among the men to see who could do it the fastest. By the time the crazy game was over—with spaghetti was flying all over the room—Danny had finished a big portion.

Another time, Sam hid a candy bar under a pile of corned beef, although by the time Danny got done slowly picking at his food, the choco-late had kind of melted together with the corned beef juice, and it didn't taste so good. The next time, Sam remembered to leave the wrapper on the candy bar to protect it.

Jesse, another Marine, started to teach him a smattering of English—"Geronimo" and "screw up" were the first words Danny learned. He was beginning to like being with this cheerful group. Then the squad was ordered back to its home base in Syracuse, New York; they would have a short furlough and then be shipped out again, to the Philippines.

"Don't worry, Danny-boy, we'll find a home

for you," Tyrone insisted. But as the army transport plane revved up its engines, Danny found himself shaking like a leaf. Where was he going this time? What would happen there?

Throughout the flight from Trieste to Syracuse, Danny was in a daze. His fists clenched, he sat tensely aboard the army transport plane, wedged between Tyrone and Sam. The squad sang songs and joked, happy to be going home even for a little while. But Danny wasn't sure what home meant. He knew only one thing—he and Tyrone would be separated.

When they finally landed, the men hooted and hollered their good-byes. Then Tyrone picked Danny up and carried him down the tarmac to a black station wagon with SAINT JOHN'S ORPHANAGE printed on its door. From inside, a pyramid of black cloth emerged. "I'm Sister Mary Theresa," the figure said. Danny looked up at the pudgy pale face bulging out of her black head-covering and spilling out over the starched white bib of her habit.

"She's going to take care of you," Tyrone said.

He gave Danny a quick hug and yelled, "so long, paratrooper," over his shoulder as he rushed off to join his squad.

St. John's was nothing more than a converted warehouse, and the nuns' efforts at decorating—with colorful pictures of suffering saints and martyrs—did little to disguise the dreariness. It was home for 120 boys between the ages of six and ten. Most of them, not having been adopted as babies, had lived in foster homes until school age and then been transferred to the institution. Danny was a special case, since he was older than the other boys, although not much bigger. A young boy could not grow on the starvation diet of a concentration camp. He had been admitted thanks to the intercession of the officials from the local Marine base, Sister Mary Theresa told him, smiling all the while, and he should consider himself lucky.

Danny didn't feel lucky at all. He felt even less lucky when he was shown to his room—a stark cell painted white, with six cots lining the wall. The windows were narrow slits so high up you had to stand on a chair to see outside. Something about this place reminded him of San Sabba. He wondered what he would see outside that window.

Sister Mary Theresa cheerfully explained that since he was older than the others, he would have to make sure the room was kept neat and the beds made. He answered, "I won't screw up."

"Holy Mother of God," Sister Mary Theresa gasped, crossing herself. "Don't ever use words like that!"

Danny was astonished at her reaction. God had a mother? That sure was news to him. Tateh had taught him that God was the Endless One, without beginning, without end. "He is, He was, He will be," Tateh had said.

But Danny was smart, and he sensed that sometimes it was better not to ask questions. This was another place where rules were made by the people who ran it. And clearly one of the rules was not to use the words that the Marines had taught him. From then on, Danny only nodded when given instructions.

The Mother Superior was the nun in charge of the orphanage. Unlike Sister Mary Theresa, who was always smiling and generally easygoing, the Mother Superior was grim and stern. She expressed dismay when Danny told her that he was a Gypsy and as such had had no religious training. Her small eyes, set deep in her pinched face, studied him from behind thick wire-rimmed glasses. "Do you know about God?"

"No," Danny lied.

"We must correct that," she said, and immediately scheduled catechism classes so that Danny could be baptized as a Catholic. Danny did not want to be a Jew, but he didn't want to be a Catholic, either. He didn't know exactly why he felt that way—perhaps it had something to do with the big black cross hanging in the catechism class. This one didn't have crooked corners like the one he knew so well, but it still made him very uncomfortable. He did not resist the religious instructions directly, so as not to get the Mother Superior angry and bring punishment on himself. But he fumbled over his lessons, pretending that he didn't understand enough English. The Mother Superior finally agreed to put the matter off for a year. Meanwhile, Danny was enrolled in a nearby junior high school.

Danny knew he was an oddball. At the orphanage, the boys stayed away from him, mimicking his thick accent behind his back. At school, out of sight of the watchful eyes of Sister Mary Theresa, they were more open with their teasing. Frank, the orphanage bully, was downright cruel, laughing loudly whenever Danny stumbled over his words in class.

His English teacher, Mrs. Dennison, was the only person who was compassionate about his problems. She'd glare at the students who dared to make fun of him; and when she caught Frank in the act, she sent him down to the principal's office for punishment.

She was a tall, attractive, middle-aged woman,

and she always wore lace collars and smelled faintly of lavender. On Danny's first day she kept him after school, gave him an elementary book in English, and showed him how to use it.

But there were so many things about English that Danny just didn't understand. One day, as he was taking his turn writing a sentence on the blackboard, he heard loud laughter from behind. It was Frank again; Danny recognized his voice without turning to look.

"Frank, one more sound out of you, and it's down to the principal's office," Mrs. Dennison admonished. "All right Danny, can you find your error?"

Danny had written on the board: THE MICE LIVED IN THE HICE. He looked at the board and at Mrs. Dennison. It was mouse, mice, so it had to be house, hice. He was sure he was right.

"Class?" Mrs. Dennison turned to the other students. "Can anyone help Danny?"

"The plural of house is houses," someone said.

Why? It didn't make any sense. Danny erased

the blackboard feeling intense frustration. English was a crazy language; he would never learn it.

But he did.

He thought he would never make any friends either.

But he did.

His first friend turned out to be an unlikely prospect—Roy, a six-year-old boy who bunked in his room.

Roy was skinny and frail, with wispy ginger hair, twinkling brown eyes, and freckles across the bridge of his nose. He wore a constant grin that revealed two front teeth with a small space in between. Danny noticed that the older boys constantly picked on Roy, and they made him do their chores—like mopping the floor or washing the dishes—in exchange for a brief chance to play on the baseball team. Danny didn't understand the game, but he could see that little Roy wasn't much of an athlete, no matter how hard he tried.

One day, egged on by Frank, Roy began to make fun of Danny in the shower. "Count the lice in your hice," he giggled, repeating words Frank had told him to say.

Danny felt anger well up within him, but he didn't react. Then Roy came closer, as the others jeered, repeating in a singsong voice, "Count the lice in your hice. . . . Count the lice in your hice."

Danny ran out of the shower, pushing Roy out of the way. The little boy lost his balance, slipped on the wet floor, and fell against the tile wall. He hit his nose, and blood immediately spurted out. Danny didn't mean to push him that hard, but Roy was so frail, so light, he just flew. The other boys quickly scattered, but Danny, seeing the little body crumpled against the wall, rushed over and tried to stop the flow of blood with his washcloth.

Sister Mary Theresa was outside dispensing towels and checking to see if the boys had scrubbed properly behind their ears. When Roy came out, still bleeding, and tears now running freely down his cheeks, she exclaimed in horror, "Roy, what happened?"

"Nuthin'," Roy mumbled.

She threw a menacing look at Danny's guilty face and pressed on, "Did someone hit you? Push you? Was it Danny?"

"No, no," said Roy. "I slipped and fell all by myself."

That night when the lights were turned out, Danny went over to Roy's bunk. "I'm sorry I pushed you . . . and thanks a lot for not telling on me," he whispered.

"It didn't hurt that bad," Roy whispered back. "I'm sorry I made fun of you."

"Okay. But I still owe you one."

"Really?" Roy seemed surprised anyone would want to do something for him. "Could you teach me to be a catcher?"

"I don't know how to play baseball," Danny answered.

"Nobody wants to teach me," Roy said mournfully.

"Well . . . I could try. . . ."

From that day on, they were practically inseparable. Roy bribed another boy, giving him a dried frog skin—the most precious possession from his cigar box of treasures—in order to sleep in the cot next to Danny's. He sneaked in an old baseball, and they tossed it back and forth from their cots.

At mealtimes, they always sat together, Danny protecting Roy when anybody tried to steal Roy's dessert. Danny also made sure that others didn't take advantage of the frail boy.

Frank didn't like this one bit. Suddenly he had lost the little slave who did his chores for him. "Roy!" he commanded one evening after supper. "Go wash the dishes."

"It's not his turn, it's your turn," Danny spoke up.

"Says who—you?" Frank laughed at Danny. Then he pointed at Roy, "Squirt, get in the kitchen before I count to ten."

Roy started to get up, but Danny grabbed his hand. "Stay put, Roy. He's not going to push you around anymore."

Frank had had enough of this. "If that little pipsqueak doesn't obey me right now, he can forget about playing ball for the whole season."

"Oh yeah?" Danny stood up.

"Yeah! Sit down." Frank punched him in the chest with his meaty fist.

That made Danny angry. Without thinking, he punched back so hard, Frank fell down just from sheer surprise. His face was red as he got up and came at Danny. But Danny's pent-up fury from all the insults he had suffered made him totally unafraid. Before Frank could even take a swing, Danny punched him again.

Frank's hand went for his lip which was starting to swell. Tears welled up in his eyes. Nothing like this had ever happened to him before. He always got his way with everybody. He looked around for reinforcements. But all the boys he had bullied for so long were not going to help him now. They were enjoying seeing someone finally stand up to Frank.

He looked again at Danny, who had his fist ready for another assault. "You'll be sorry," he muttered and left the room.

That evening Roy didn't wash the dishes,

and when it came time for baseball, Danny was there to make sure Frank let Roy play.

And suddenly everyone deferred to Danny. He was the oldest boy in the orphanage, and now, at last, he was treated like a respected senior. Roy was in his glory to be under Danny's protection.

One night, Danny was awakened by Roy shaking him hysterically.

"What's the matter?" Danny muttered sleepily.

"Danny, Danny . . . I'm scared . . . " Roy whispered.

"Of what?"

"Of that!" Roy shuddered. A low rumbling thunder could be heard in the distance.

"Oh, that's nothing," Danny assured him. "That's just angels bowling up in heaven."

"What?"

"Yes, the noise is just their bowling ball rolling over the clouds."

"Wow? Really? That's all?"

"That's all. Didn't you know that?"

"No, nobody told me."

"So, now I told you, and you don't have to be afraid. Get back to bed and go to sleep."

Roy reluctantly got into his own bed and anxiously looked up at the window where lightning had just flashed.

Danny looked up at the window, too. It wasn't raining yet, but, from the sound of the thunder, he could guess a big storm was brewing. "Bet one of them drops it soon."

"Drops what, Danny?" Roy asked. "The bowling ball?"

"No, his little bag." In the dark, Danny knew Roy couldn't see the mischievous grin on his face.

"What little bag?"

"Don't you know about the angels and their little bags?" Danny was beginning to like his new role as storyteller.

"No," Roy said mournfully. "Nobody told me about that, either."

"Well, there are millions and millions of

angels up there in heaven, and they are small just like us—children angels."

"Small, like me?"

"Some are even smaller. And each one carries a little bag over his shoulder with a raindrop in it."

"And they drop them down?"

"Yes, but it's always a big problem, because no angel wants to be the first."

"That's a long way to drop something. Suppose you miss?" Roy understood this problem very well.

"Yeah, it's hard to be first—you get scared you might do it wrong. But somebody has to be the one to start, or it won't rain."

"If I were an angel, I could never go first. Could you, Danny?" And without waiting for an answer he went on. "Yes, you could do it. You would be the first one, Danny. You're brave . . . but I would follow you."

And just then a huge raindrop hit the windowpane, and then another, and another and another.

Roy giggled. "Do they have little bags for snow, too?"

"Oh no, snow is just the stuff they sweep from the porch of heaven."

"Snow is dirt? But it's white!"

"Everything in heaven is white, even dirt."

"Wow!" Roy was impressed. "How do you know all this about the angels, Danny?"

"My sis—" Danny stopped himself. He almost said, "my sister, Rachel." But he got this deep pain in his stomach, and he couldn't say it. He couldn't tell Roy that the angel stories came from the book that Rachel had read to him. He rolled over with his back to Roy and just muttered, "I read it somewhere."

"Oh wow, Danny! Can you tell me more?"

Danny didn't answer. He just pulled the thin blanket over his shoulders. Suddenly his little game was spoiled. He felt very sad and he didn't want to talk to Roy anymore.

"Oh please, Danny, please! . . ." Little Roy could be quite persistent when he wanted something.

"Not tonight."

"Tomorrow night?"

"I don't know any more stories."

"Maybe you could read me one." Roy was not easily put off; and his voice pleaded so sweetly, it was impossible for Danny to turn him down.

"Pipe down!" That came from Harry, a boy in another bunk who also had been awakened by the thunder. "Let's get some shut-eye!"

To keep peace, Danny finally sighed, "Roy, if you go to sleep now, tomorrow I'll read you a story."

There was silence for a minute. And then he heard another whisper from Roy's bunk. "What do they do with the little bags?"

"Stuff them down the throats of loud-mouths!" Harry was really mad now.

That did it. Roy finally shut up. But if his silence brought peace to Harry, it didn't help Danny much. The angel stories had brought a flood of memories, and he didn't fall asleep again. He lay the rest of the night, crying softly, feeling as if the rain and the angels were crying with him.

* * *

By the next night, Roy had traded another of his treasures for a flashlight so Danny could read him a story after Sister Mary Theresa turned out the lights.

And that's how it began. Danny would spend hours in the meager orphanage library, trying to find interesting books for Roy.

One day, Danny found a copy of Andersen's fairy tales. He picked up the richly illustrated book and began leafing through it excitedly. Then he stopped. He was looking at a picture of Satan and his disciples flying through the clouds with their mirror. As he stared at the drawing, his eyes started to burn. He remembered Rachel reading this story to him, and that old hurt came back again. All those beautiful memories that were dead now, along with all the people who were also dead. That was so long ago. That was when he was a Jew. That was a time that no longer existed.

But he would not allow himself to cry. He slammed the cover shut and shoved the book back on the shelf so hard it fell behind the book rack.

The first Sunday of every month was the worst day at the orphanage. It was bad enough that, as usual, they had to get up extra early for the 6 A.M. service at the nearby church; the pastor didn't like them taking up the pews during the more popular masses later on. But then, when they came back, they had to get things ready for the prospective parents' communion breakfast. Most of the boys dreaded the emotional roller coaster of the day—high hopes, followed by hopes crushed. But the Mother Superior was in her glory. She would always deliver a long address to the assembled couples, sanctifying the deed of giving an unfortunate orphan a home, dramatizing the rewards such a generous act would bring in heaven. Then the boys marched in, lining up four-deep on the platform, like so much merchandise on display. They sang hymns while the adults munched on their eggs and toast, studying them with interest. By the time breakfast was over, at least one of the boys would have a new set of parents. He was the lucky one; the others were devastated.

During the time that he had been at St. John's, Danny had often overheard people saying that he was too old to be adopted. He was glad of it. He had settled into a routine; he didn't want things to change again. He was doing well in school, he had almost lost his accent, and he was accepted by everyone. The only thing worrying him was that little Roy might be taken away.

Like so many of the boys, Roy watched the couples with desperate eyes, hoping that this would be his lucky day. He wanted to be adopted very badly, and he constantly fantasized what kind of a home he might someday have. He told Danny that he was abandoned as a baby and never knew his parents.

"Do you remember your mommy and daddy, Danny?" he once asked.

Of course Danny did. But he told Roy curtly, "I don't want to talk about it."

The nights after the Sunday breakfasts, Roy

had nightmares and sometimes wet his bed. This embarrassed him dreadfully, and he knew what the punishment for bed-wetting would be. If any boy was caught, he got no dinner and had to stand in the dining hall with a sign hanging from his neck: I WET MY BED.

Several times Danny sneaked fresh linens from the hall closet while the others were sleeping and helped Roy remake the bed before Sister Mary Theresa could find out. The wet sheet was tucked into the springs until the next dirty-laundry pickup.

One Sunday night Danny was awakened by a whisper in his ear, "Danny, Danny . . . help me . . . I wet my bed."

"Oh no, Roy, not again." Sleepily, Danny stumbled out of bed and headed to the linen closet. But when he reached inside, the shelf was bare. Momentarily, he panicked. Then, quietly, he returned to the room. "Just keep your mouth shut," he commanded Roy as he stripped off the wet sheet and switched it with his own.

"But you'll get punished," Roy muttered.

"Go to sleep," Danny ordered gruffly, sliding into the damp bed. "You're too skinny to miss dinner again."

Dozing off, he heard Roy's soft voice. "Danny—"

"Now what?"

"Maybe we'll get adopted together."

"Maybe."

Danny's worst time at the orphanage was the evening when he had to stand in the dining hall with that awful sign around his neck.

At the close of the school year, there was a recital in the auditorium, and Mrs. Dennison had Danny memorize a poem.

"Don't be afraid, Danny—your English is very good now. I'll be sitting in the first row. If you get scared, just look at me. I'll be whispering the words along with you."

But he didn't need to look at her as he recited without an accent:

If you can dream—and not make dreams your master;

If you can think—and not make thoughts
your aim,
If you can meet with Triumph and Disaster
And treat those two impostors just the same; . . .

The audience applauded; Danny liked the sound. That night he told Roy all about it. Roy had memorized the poem, too. He didn't have much choice, since that's all Danny had read to him for weeks now, until they both knew it perfectly.

Danny urged Roy to recite the poem at the next communion breakfast. Roy did, and got an enthusiastic response—even the Mother Superior smiled. One couple applauded more loudly than the others.

After breakfast, Danny was the first to spot them conferring with the Mother Superior as the boys cleared the dishes. He guessed it—they wanted to adopt Roy.

Danny had to hide his feelings of sadness when he looked at Roy's happy face. He had to admit he liked the looks of Roy's parents—they were chubby and had wide grins on their round, pink faces. They would be good parents for skinny little Roy; they'd fatten him up for sure. He told Roy that as he helped him pack. It didn't take long; everything Roy owned fit in his cigar box. His new parents were waiting downstairs.

Roy bounced toward the door. Danny could not move. He felt short of breath, and he had a sinking sensation, as if he were going deeper underwater and didn't have the strength to come up for air.

Suddenly, Roy turned around, a worried expression on his face. "Danny, do you think we could sneak a sheet out of the closet, just one, and fold it real small so it fits in the cigar box, you know, just in case . . ."

"Don't worry," Danny reassured him. "It won't happen again. You'll have a new father, a new mother, a nice house, and a room of your own. You won't have nightmares anymore. You'll sleep well."

"But what do I do if . . . " begged Roy.

"Well, just tell your mother to read you a story." Then he commanded sharply, "Come on!"

He carried Roy's cigar box downstairs, where the waiting parents were still smiling. As they led him toward their car, Roy broke away and rushed back. He threw his arms around Danny in a tight hug. His frail body shook with violent sobs. "I love you, Danny—I'll never, ever forget you."

Danny stood rooted to the spot. When the car disappeared from view, he was still there. And the lump in his throat wouldn't go away.

When night fell Danny could not go to sleep. The bed next to his was empty. No one was asking him to read a story. He thought his heart would break.

He didn't sleep that night or the next or the next. His worn-out appearance worried Mrs. Dennison, who sent him home from school with a note that he was ill and should have a check-up.

The Mother Superior knew better. She had seen other boys grieve over the loss of a friend who was adopted, but she had to admit that Danny's reaction was extreme.

She called him into her office. "You are older, Danny, and you should know better than to act this way, just because one of the boys was adopted."

Roy wasn't one of the boys, Danny wanted to scream, he was my best friend. But he said nothing. He only stared.

"Danny, why are you acting this way?"

Again, Danny said nothing. If he said anything, he'd have to say everything, and that he couldn't do. He couldn't tell her that he had once been a Jewish boy named Moishe, who had seen the life drained out of his mother in a matter of days, who had seen his father's body dragged away like a sack of garbage, who had a sister named Rachel. . . . He could never begin to tell her what it felt like to lose Rachel. And now Roy . . .

His silence only irritated the Mother Superior. She told him that if he was going to sulk, he should go to his room without supper. Danny didn't care. He had no appetite anyway.

By Friday, he could stand it no longer. He went down to the Mother Superior's office and broke his silence. "Please," he pleaded, "can I have Roy's address so I can write him a letter?"

But the Mother Superior just shook her head. "That is information we never give out, Danny. You know that."

"But he was my best friend—"

"I know. But often in life we have to put such temporal attachments aside and get on with what is important."

Nothing else was important as far as Danny was concerned. This woman would never understand that. Inside he felt very angry. Who was she to lecture him about attachments? What did she know about losing someone you loved? He was sure that the Mother Superior had never been small or frightened. If she had ever been a child, if she had ever had a friend, she couldn't be so mean to him now.

He walked out of her office and kept on walking. He wanted to get away from this place. He would never, ever see Roy again. The thought was so painful, so excruciating, that he simply could not bear it.

He started to run—down the hall and out the door, and he kept on running.

He ran and ran until he was exhausted. He sat down on a park bench and must have fallen asleep from exhaustion. When he woke up, he was stiff and shivering.

He didn't know what to do, and then he saw a policeman coming his way. The Mother Superior must have reported him as a runaway.

He got up quickly, stumbled over an untied shoelace, tucked it in his shoe, fearful that the policeman would notice him if he took the time to tie it.

He started walking away quickly; then, as he imagined himself being forcefully returned to the orphanage, he started to run again.

Crossing an empty lot, he stumbled and fell in the mud, but he didn't care. He just got up and kept on running.

Finally, his young body gave out. He could run no longer, but he could still keep on moving and so he did, walking slower and slower as his muscles shut down from complete exhaustion.

He thought he would just lie down and die. Surely he could bear this no longer. He started to cry again, shaken by violent sobs of complete despair.

And then he heard a familiar sound coming from a distance.

He could hardly believe it. He lifted his head, trying to figure out where it was coming from.

It was coming from a big building at end of the street. He started walking in that direction.

The windows of this building glowed with a warm light that beckoned to him. Suddenly, he knew that if he reached the light he would be saved. At that moment, he believed it with all his heart, and he used the last ounce of strength to move his tired, aching body toward those beautiful lights.

As he got closer the lights got more and more blurry; he couldn't see them clearly because hot tears were streaming down his face.

Finally—it seemed like it took forever—he reached the doors of the building and pushed them open.

"*Leha Dodi, Likrat Kala,*" the voices of the men boomed. "Come, my Beloved, let's meet the bride, come let's greet the Sabbath." This was the song Moishe knew so well—the song he used to sing in the synagogue every Friday evening at sundown.

"Feel not ashamed, be not humiliated. . . . Why are you downcast? Why do you cry? . . . The city that is destroyed will be rebuilt on the hilltop."

At the end of the song, as was the custom, the men turned around to face the door and bowed, greeting the Sabbath bride: "*Leha Dodi, Likrat Kala, p'nay Shabbat n'kablah . . .*"

But that evening, when the men of Synagogue B'nai David turned around to greet the Sabbath bride, they saw not a bride, but a small boy standing in the doorway. He was covered with mud, and tears were streaming down his face.

The rabbi—a short man with a thick red beard and a head full of curly red hair—walked down the aisle and put his arm around the boy.

"What are you doing here?"

Danny couldn't answer because the lump in his throat wouldn't let him speak.

"Where are your parents?"

Danny, sobbing uncontrollably now, pulled up his torn shirtsleeve and exposed the number on his arm.

Tears appeared in the rabbi's eyes. He knew that people with numbers tattooed on their arms had been in concentration camps and had probably lost everyone they loved. "Whatever is wrong, we will make it right," he said softly. "This is your family—all of us here." He took Danny by the hand.

Danny let himself be led. He was crying still, but he didn't feel sad anymore.

That night, the rabbi brought him into a home that reminded him of his own so long ago. There was a lace tablecloth on the table and candles shining with a bright beautiful light.

Suddenly, the hungry spot in the middle of him didn't feel so empty anymore. Suddenly, he felt like someone had rolled the clock backward, and he was back to the time when things were happy, and Mameh and Rachel were baking challah in the kitchen.

That night Danny became Moishe again, and he said the blessing over the challah like Tateh had taught him. The rabbi's wife had baked the bread and prepared the meal with the help of her seven daughters, all of whom wanted to help Moishe fill his plate. He laughed at the mountain of food before him.

When the dinner was over the rabbi took him gently aside, and Moishe told him the whole story, beginning with when the Nazis burned down the synagogue and ending with little Roy's adoption.

The rabbi listened patiently and nodded. And when he was through, they just sat there silently for a long time.

Then the rabbi smiled. "As you see, Moishe, we have seven daughters and no sons. It appears there is a job here you could fill."

"You mean . . . ?" Moishe couldn't finish.

"I would like you to be my son."

Moishe couldn't believe it. But it was true.

His story would have a happy ending.

After the Sabbath was over, the rabbi went to visit the Mother Superior. He was a man well versed in Talmudic debate, and the Mother Superior was no match for him. When he left, the rabbi had not only initiated the adoption process, but he also had Roy's address and phone number to give to Danny.

The next Sabbath was the happiest Moishe had had since his nightmare began. He sang "*Leha Dodi*" the loudest of anybody in the synagogue. He was holding the hand of his best friend, Roy, who had come to spend this Sabbath with him. Nothing could separate them now. They both had found families who wanted them and loved them, and they would be friends forever.

Of course, whenever Roy stayed over, he always asked Moishe to read him a story. And one day, Moishe read him the story of Satan's mirror. It was a story with a happy ending.

Kay—the little boy who had gotten a piece

of the mirror in his heart so that it turned to ice—had had many terrible adventures. But at the end, his friend Gerda, who loved him very much, found him. She cried such hot tears that they fell on his heart and thawed the ice and melted the piece of mirror in it.

And then Moishe explained to Roy that he had once lived in a country where many, many pieces of Satan's mirror had fallen. All the people in that country became ugly and mean and did terrible things to other people.

He even suspected that maybe a very tiny piece had turned his heart to ice, just as had happened to Kay. But the candles of the Sabbath had burned so brightly that they had melted the ice. And, like Kay and Gerda, he and Roy would live happily ever after.

Roy liked that part the best. And when Moishe got to that point, he always said:

"The end."